Church Member's Handbook

Revised Edition

Joe T. Odle

REV. R.E. GROVES
3132 JEFFLAND RD.
BALTIMORE, MD 21207

BROADMAN PRESS
Nashville, Tennessee

© Copyright 1962 • BROADMAN PRESS
Nashville, Tennessee

All rights reserved
International copyright secured

ISBN: 0-8054-9401-4
4294-01

Printed in the United States of America

Foreword

Since I first entered the pastorate, I often have felt the need for a small book on church membership to place in the hands of members to help them know the meaning of their membership and understand the doctrines and polity of Baptists. Being unable to find such a book, I decided to prepare one. Several months ago an edition was published privately, and I quickly found that other pastors and church workers felt the same need. Orders came in from a number of states, and several thousand copies were sold. For such a response I am humbly grateful to the Lord, and now that larger opportunity comes for the little book through its publication by Broadman Press, my prayer is that it may have a useful ministry in the work of many of our churches.

The book is necessarily brief, many things being omitted; but an effort has been made to discuss the more important things a member should know. It should be studied with Bible in hand since, in order to save space, most Bible references are given but not quoted. If the book proves a blessing in that it helps someone to be a better Baptist, its purpose shall have been achieved.

JOE T. ODLE

June, 1941

Foreword to Revised Edition

More than twenty years have passed since the first edition of this book was published. During that time over one million copies have been printed, and the book has been used in churches throughout the United States and in mission fields around the world. Portions of the material have been translated into at least five foreign languages, and a Chinese edition was published in Hong Kong.

There have come numerous reports of souls won to the Lord, of saved persons being led into church membership, and of members rededicating their lives because of the book. Thousands of pastors have distributed it, and hundreds of thousands of new church members have studied it either individually or in new member classes.

For the widespread ministry the Lord has given the book, I am humbly grateful. My prayer is that this revised edition will find an even larger place of service as it assists pastors in teaching new members the true meaning of membership in a Baptist church. If it does this, it will continue to accomplish the purpose for which it was prepared.

JOE T. ODLE

September, 1962

Contents

1. The Meaning of Church Membership 7

2. The Church Covenant 9

3. Christian Growth 11

4. Baptist History 13

5. Baptist Doctrine 19

6. Baptists and Other Denominations 25

7. God's Plan of Church Finance 27

8. Baptist Churches at Work 30

1. The Meaning of Church Membership

"I'm now a member of a Baptist church."

Millions of persons utter these words with a joy in their hearts that is inexpressible. They have found Christ as Saviour, their sins are forgiven, and there is peace in their souls. As Christians they have obeyed the Lord's command to follow him in baptism and unite with his church; they have found great happiness in this new relationship.

Many, however, who speak those words fail to comprehend their significance. Sometimes they live for many years without ever seeming to learn the real meaning of membership. This should not be true. Every member should know the seriousness and sacredness of his commitment. It is surprising that so many hold membership without realizing their privileges and opportunities or accepting their obligations. Surely this is not because of a determination to be indifferent. They have not been brought face to face with the real meaning of church membership, nor have they had its various aspects laid on their hearts. In this chapter and throughout this booklet, we seek to set forth some of these things.

Just what is this organization to which you belong? It is a New Testament church. Dr. George W. McDaniel defined a local church as "an organized body of baptized believers equal in rank and privileges, administering its affairs under the headship of Christ, united in the belief of what He has taught, covenanting together to do what He has commanded, and co-operating with other like bodies in Kingdom movements" (*The Churches of the New Testament*, p. 23).

The church of the Lord Jesus Christ is the greatest institution that the world has ever known. Christ established it during his personal ministry, and he is its Head (Matt. 16:18; Eph. 5:23; Col. 1:18). He promised that he would be with it through the ages and that the gates of hell should not prevail against it (Matt. 16:18; 28:20). To it he gave the Great Commission and the ordinances, and for it he went to the cross (Matt. 28:19-20; 1 Cor. 11:23-26; Eph. 5:25). He loved the church, and he wants his churches to honor and glorify him as his representatives on the earth (Eph. 3:21; 5:25-27).

The Lord's churches have the greatest task ever assigned to any individual or group in the world's history—carrying the glorious gospel of Christ the Saviour to every nation and tongue. No other commission like that has ever been given or will ever be given. In carrying out this work, the churches have done more for the world than all the governments ever organized, all the other institutions ever established, or all the armies ever assembled. World history has been changed by the work of Christ through his churches.

We see then that we have a great privilege in being members of Baptist churches. They are churches with a glorious beginning, a blood-written history, an illustrious present, and a future as bright as the promises of God. They are churches that have held true to God's Word through persecution and tribulation and whose members have been numbered among the faithful. They are churches that today have a membership of more than twenty-five million, and are growing rapidly as they carry the true gospel message to a lost world. Truly it is a privilege to be a member of a Baptist church.

Membership also brings us great opportunities. These include opportunity for fellowship in the finest company that can be found and opportunity for Christian growth, development, and training through the various departments of the church organization. We have opportunity for Christian service through the church in the name of Christ to those at home and around the globe. Where else can we find such opportunities to live for God and our fellow men?

Membership places upon us an inescapable obligation—an obligation to make the church and its work first in our lives. It is an obligation to use our time and our talents for the glory of God, an obligation to support the work with our presence, our influence, and our means. Churches are never stronger than their membership; and a membership of worldly, careless, negligent, stunted Christians will prevent a church from accomplishing much for the Lord. There is need for every member to be consecrated, trained, and enlisted in active service. We are under obligation to be the very best members possible under the leading of the Lord.

We see then that membership is a privilege and an opportunity that entails great obligations. Too many members have not learned these things. Their churches mean little to them, and they mean little to their churches. Dr. E. P. Alldredge, who for many years served as secretary of the Department of Survey, Statistics, and Information of the Baptist Sunday School Board, once said that 60 per cent of the members of the average church were unenlisted. That condition must be changed. Won't you help change it by making your membership really count for Christ?

2. The Church Covenant

The church covenant is a voluntary agreement by members of a Baptist church whereby they promise to conduct their lives in such a way as to glorify God and promote the ongoing of his church. Every member should study it carefully, refer to it often, and seek to live by it. It clearly outlines the obligations of church membership. The form of covenant in wide use in Baptist churches is as follows:

Covenant

Having been led, as we believe, by the Spirit of God, to receive the Lord Jesus Christ as our Saviour, and on the profession of our faith, having been baptized in the name of the Father, and of the Son, and of the Holy Ghost, we do now in the presence of God, angels, and this assembly, most solemnly and joyfully enter into covenant with one another, as one body in Christ.

We engage, therefore, by the aid of the Holy Spirit, to walk together in Christian love; to strive for the advancement of this church, in knowledge, holiness, and comfort; to promote its prosperity and spirituality; to sustain its worship, ordinances, discipline, and doctrines; to contribute cheerfully and regularly to the support of the ministry, the expenses of the church, the relief of the poor, and the spread of the gospel through all nations.

We also engage to maintain family and secret devotions; to religiously educate our children; to seek the salvation of our kindred and acquaintances; to walk circumspectly in the world; to be just in our dealings; faithful in our engagements, and exemplary in our deportment; to avoid all tattling, backbiting, and excessive anger; to abstain from the sale and use of intoxicating drinks as a beverage; and to be zealous in our efforts to advance the kingdom of our Saviour.

We further engage to watch over one another in brotherly love; to remember each other in prayer; to aid each other in sickness and distress; to cultivate Christian sympathy in feeling and courtesy in speech; to be slow to take offense, but always ready for reconciliation, and mindful of the rules of our Saviour to secure it without delay.

We moreover engage that when we remove from this place we will, as soon as possible, unite with some other church, where we can carry out the spirit of this covenant and the principles of God's Word.

Basis of Covenant

The obligations of church membership outlined in the covenant are all scriptural, as may be seen from the following study.

I. Salvation and Baptism (John 1:11-12; Matt. 28:19-20).

II. Duties to the Church
1. To walk together in Christian love (John 13:34-35).
2. To strive for the advancement of the church and promote its prosperity and spirituality (Phil. 1:27; 2 Tim. 2:15; 2 Cor. 7:1; 2 Peter 3:11).
3. To sustain its worship, ordinances, discipline, and doctrine (Heb. 10:25; Matt. 28:19; 1 Cor. 11:23-26; Jude 3).
4. To give it pre-eminence in my life (Matt. 6:33).
5. To contribute cheerfully and regularly (1 Cor. 16:2; 2 Cor. 8:6-7).
6. To carry my membership when I move and be active in church work wherever I live (Acts 11:19-21; 18:24-28).

III. Duties in Personal Christian Living
1. To maintain family and secret devotions (1 Thess. 5:17-18; Acts 17:11).
2. To religiously educate the children (2 Tim. 3:15; Deut. 6:4-7).
3. To seek the salvation of the lost (Acts 1:8; Matt. 4:19; Psalm 126:5-6; Prov. 11:30).
4. To walk circumspectly in the world, and to be just in our dealings, faithful in our engagements, and exemplary in our deportment (Eph. 5:15; Phil. 2:14-15; 1 Peter 2:11-12).
5. To avoid gossip and excessive anger (Eph. 4:31; 1 Peter 2:21; Col. 3:8; James 3:1-2).
6. To abstain from sale or use of liquors. (Eph. 5:18; Hab. 2:15).
7. To be zealous in our efforts for Christ (Titus 2:14).

IV. Duties to Fellow Members
1. To watch over one another in love (1 Peter 1:22).
2. To pray for one another (James 5:16).
3. To aid in sickness and distress (Gal. 6:2; James 2:14-17).
4. To cultivate sympathy and courtesy (1 Peter 3:8).
5. To be slow to take offense, always ready for reconciliation (Eph. 4:30-32).

3. Christian Growth

Every child of God should desire to grow spiritually. This is scriptural, for 2 Peter 3:18 says, "Grow in grace." When we are saved, we do not immediately become full-grown Christians but are only "babes in Christ." As "babes" we are commanded to "grow." To remain a "babe" is a shame and a tragedy. Only by growing spiritually can we please God and glorify him in our lives.

How can a Christian grow in grace? A large book, or a series of sermons could be written on this subject, so we cannot give a comprehensive discussion here. The following principles, however, can be outlined.

1. Be sure that you are born again. Certainly you cannot grow spiritually if you are not a child of God. The Lord said, "Ye must be born again." We are born again when we repent of sin and commit ourselves to Christ as our personal Lord and Saviour. Make sure of your salvation.

2. Unite with one of the Lord's churches, and go to work for him. Christ loved the church and gave himself for it. He wants us to love it and give ourselves to it. You cannot expect to grow spiritually if you do not obey the Lord's first command to you as a Christian—to unite with his church. You cannot live as good a Christian life outside the church as in it. Make your church the most important interest of your life. Attend the services, and participate in the activities. Matthew 6:33 says, "Seek ye first" the work of the Lord. We must do this to grow.

3. Cultivate your devotional life through Bible study and prayer. The Bible is God's Word to us. Read it daily. Read it through. Read it by books and by subjects. The more you read it, the more it will mean to you. You will thus be better equipped for service to the Lord. Prayer is God's child in conversation with him. The Bible says, "Pray without ceasing." Pray daily. Pray about everything. Pray as you work. Have a secret place of prayer. Establish a family altar in your home—a time when all the family is gathered together for Bible reading and prayer. We cannot grow spiritually if we do not develop the devotional life.

4. Make much of Christian fellowship. Let you closest friendships be with other Christians. Visit their homes and invite them to your home. Such fellowship is rich and blessed and will be a great strength for you in resisting temptation and growing spiritually.

5. Separate yourself from the world (2 Cor. 6:14-18). The world is against God (1 John 2:15-17). We are in the world, but we must not be of the world. Let us separate ourselves from everything that is worldly, everything that would hinder our work for Christ. As long as we hold on to worldly things we cannot grow spiritually.

6. Use and cultivate your talents for the Lord. Every Christian has abilities which he can use for God. Use your ability to speak, to sing, to handle business, to bring joy to needy hearts, to teach, to organize, or whatever your talent may be. The church needs that which each member can do. Dedicate yourself to Christ today (1 Cor. 12:12-31).

7. Read good books and other Christian literature. Every home should have religious books and periodicals. Subscribe for the denominational weekly paper and mission journals. Do not let the wrong type of books and other literature have a place in your home.

8. Be honest toward God in the use of your money. Every Christian's income belongs to God. At least a tenth of it should be brought to God's house regularly. If you are dishonest toward God in matters relating to money, your spiritual growth will be stunted. Study carefully chapter 7 of this book.

9. Exercise self-control. Satan is ever seeking to hinder our Christian lives and the Lord's work by bringing jealousy, ill-temper, and selfishness into our hearts. Church work has often been hindered by some Christian who sought to be "bossy" or was non-co-operative. Such a spirit is of the devil. If it appears in your life, destroy it by Bible study and prayer.

10. Seek the counsel and help of your pastor. He is one of the best friends you can have. God has set him in the church to aid you, to teach you, and to lead you. Confide in him. Work with him. When you are in trouble, he will be ready to help you. When you are tempted, he will fight with you in your battle with Satan. When you need spiritual counsel or guidance, you will find no better earthly friend than your pastor. As you walk with him, you will be walking closer to God; seek his fellowship.

11. Live for Christ one day at a time. Each morning you awake to find that God has given you a new day to use for him. Live for him every minute of it—in your business, at your job, in your home, in your social relationships, and wherever you are. Live for him in the quiet moments, those times when you are alone. This does not mean that you will neglect the responsibilities of your business or home, but it does mean that you will so live that the spirit of Christ is manifested in your life.

Live for Christ twenty-four hours a day. If you fail, as you sometimes will, confess your sin in repentance and ask God to help you overcome it. Sometimes Christians give up when they fail once. That is not God's way. His Word says, "If we confess our sins, he is faithful and just to forgive us our sins, and to cleanse us from all unrighteousness" (1 John 1:9). Peter denied the Lord, but he did not turn away in despair. He came to the Lord in repentance and was forgiven. Later he became the mighty preacher of Pentecost. Do your best to resist the tempter; but if you sometimes fail, do not give up. Get up, get right, and go on. As you live for Christ one day at a time, you will soon be living weeks and months and years for him. This is the way of victorious living.

12. Win others to Christ. The greatest work in the world is soul-winning. Every Christian can and should bring others to the Saviour. This work saves souls from hell, brings joy on earth and in heaven, and is the greatest means of Christian growth. Dedicate yourself to it today, and ask God to guide you. Pray for lost persons that you know. As God leads you, talk to them about their spiritual needs. Tell them about your own experience of salvation. This was Paul's method. Everywhere he went, he gave testimony of his glorious conversion. Use the Bible in talking to the lost. Pray with them. Lead them to pray for themselves. When they have found the Saviour, lead them to confess him openly and unite with the church. This work will give you the greatest joy you have known as a Christian (Psalm 126:5-6).

Other things could be said about growing in the spiritual life, but space does not permit. Allow the Holy Spirit to guide you, and he will lead you into greater spiritual knowledge and blessings day by day. Spiritual growth is possible. Seek it.

4. Baptist History

Baptist churches seek to follow the pattern of Christ's church in the New Testament. Baptists thus believe that their history began with Christ and the apostles. This often has been proclaimed by Baptist historians and preachers. It is one of the most glorious claims ever made for any church. Most Baptists believe that both the Bible and history substantiate its truth.

What is the meaning of such a claim for Baptists? It does not mean that the Baptist denomination can be traced by name back to Christ. Also, it does not mean that there has been found an unbroken chain of baptisms, churches, or ministers. It does mean that from the days of Christ until now, no date can be cited, no place designated, and no founder named, with the positive assertion, "This is where Baptists began!" It also means that in every age from New Testament days until the present time, Christ's church has continued to exist. There have been churches holding essential New Testament principles such as those held by Baptists today.

In a book such as this we can give only a brief outline of the beginning and history of Baptists. If the reader desires to make further study, there are numerous splendid volumes available. Consult the church librarian or the pastor concerning them.

I. The Beginning of the New Testament Church

1. Christ established his church during his personal ministry here on the earth. This is one of the things which he definitely said he would do: "Upon this rock I will build my church; and the gates of hell shall not prevail against it" (Matt. 16:18). Before Christ left the earth, he stated that the work he had come to do was finished (John 17:4; 19:30).

The first members were the apostles (1 Cor. 12:28). Jesus took these men, who had been baptized by John the Baptist, and formed them into his church. Before he left the earth, this church had a membership of about 120 (Acts 1:15), an organization, the ordinances, a commission, and a treasurer. On Pentecost the three thousand saved and baptized were "added" to the church, which was already in existence. This church was a local, visible body.

2. In the Greek New Testament the word translated "church" is *ekklēsia*. George W. McDaniel, in his book, *The Churches of the New Testament*, said that it is used 109 times to refer to the Lord's church. He held that in 93 cases it designates a local church; in 14 cases, the church as an institution; and twice, all of the saved together in glory (pp. 296-99).

When the word "church" is used of an institution, it does not mean one big universal church but an institution made up of individual churches. When we speak of "the home" or "the school" we do not mean one big universal home or school. Nor is there one big church. The New Testament never speaks of a group of churches as "the church," nor are the words "universal" or "invisible" used with reference to the church anywhere in the New Testament. If there is a sense in which all of the saved make up a universal, invisible church, it has no real existence until it is assembled in glory.

The way Jesus used the word *ekklēsia* or church also reveals that the church he established was a local, visible body. He used the word 22 times: 3 times in Matthew and 19 times in Revelation. In 21 of those 22 uses Jesus clearly was speaking of a local church. In the other use (Matt. 16:18), he said, "I will build my church." There is no reason to believe that he was thinking of something altogether different from the local, visible body of which he spoke in all of the other references. Evidently here he was thinking of the church as the institution which he was about to establish. When that institution is an actual reality, however, it exists as local, visible bodies.[1]

3. Churches like this first church have continued to exist from that day to the present time. Christ promised that they would not cease to exist. He said that "the gates of hell shall not prevail against" his church (Matt. 16:18). He said that it would be in the world to the end of the age (Matt. 28:20). If the words of Jesus were true (and we know that they were), then there have been New Testament churches in existence in every age since Jesus spoke. They will continue to be in the world until he comes again. In the brief historical sketch in section III of this chapter, we show how Christ's promise did not fail.

II. Finding New Testament Churches Today

Since New Testament churches, like those set up by our Lord, are in the world today, how may they be identified?

1. New Testament churches must have four things true concerning their origin and doctrine. (1) They must have the right founder—Jesus Christ. (2) They must have been founded in the right place—in Palestine, where Christ lived. (3) They must have been founded at the right time—during the earthly ministry of Jesus. (4) They must be teaching the doctrines the Lord gave his church in the New Testament.

Churches which cannot meet these conditions can hardly be the churches the Lord established. Can any churches meet such requirements? Where did the various denominations begin? The following table, showing the origin of some of the denominations, is prepared from the statements of historians. Similar facts could be given concerning every other denomination except Baptists.

Denomination	Founder	Place	Date
Roman Catholic	Pope Leo I	Rome	440[2]

[1]Some Southern Baptists hold that "church" is sometimes used in the New Testament in a universal sense. For presentation of this view, see "Church," *Encyclopedia of Southern Baptists*, I, 272-76.

[2]Roman Catholicism was centuries in developing. Before Leo I, the popes (or bishops of Rome) had claimed for themselves a position of special importance in the Christian churches. Leo, however, more clearly and effectively than his predecessors, claimed that the pope was head of all the churches. Subsequent popes continued this claim, which is the distinguishing mark of Romanism.

Lutheran	Martin Luther	Germany	1520
Episcopal	King Henry VIII	England	1534
Presbyterian	John Calvin	Switzerland	1536
Congregational	R. Browne	England	1581
Methodist	John Wesley	England	1740
Disciples (Church of Christ)	Alexander Campbell	U. S. A.	1827
Mormon	Joseph Smith	U. S. A.	1830
Christian Scientist	Mary B. Eddy	U. S. A.	1879

2. A study of this historical table will quickly reveal that it would be difficult for any of these denominations to prove that its churches are the true New Testament churches established by the Lord while he was here. Even if historical records are not considered, the doctrinal test is enough. For example, how can churches which teach sprinkling for baptism or sprinkling of babies, neither of which is found in the New Testament, claim that they are true New Testament churches?

3. Does this mean that Christ's promise of perpetuity did fail and that there are no true New Testament churches in the world? Baptists do not accept such a conclusion. They believe that their churches are New Testament churches because of their doctrines, their organization, and their practices. Many of them also believe that Baptists have a historical relationship with churches in every age since Christ.

Some Baptists believe that the doctrinal claim is all that is necessary—that the authentication of a Baptist church is its acceptance of the New Testament as its sole and final authority. Many of these, including numerous modern scholars, say that Baptist history can only be traced back to the Reformation period; but they recognize that Baptist principles do reach back to Christ.

Other Baptists, and others who are not Baptists, believe that there is a kinship between the Baptists of today and groups through the ages who have held to basic New Testament truth. The following quotations reveal this position:

John T. Christian (Baptist): "I have no question in my own mind that there has been a historical succession of Baptists from the days of Christ to the present time" (*A History of the Baptists,* pp. 5-6).

George W. McDaniel (Baptist): "Baptists are justly proud of their parentage—the New Testament. They have an ancient and scriptural origin. . . . There is no personality this side of Jesus Christ who is a satisfactory explanation of their origin" *(The People Called Baptists).*

Alexander Campbell (Disciple or Church of Christ): "The Baptists can trace their origin to Apostolic times and can produce unequivocal testimony of their existence in every century down to the present time" (Debate with Walker).

John C. Ridpath (Methodist): "I should not readily admit that there was a Baptist *church* as far back as A.D. 100, though without doubt there were Baptists then, as all Christians were then Baptists" (quoted from W. A. Jarrel, *Baptist Church Perpetuity,* p. 59). If all Christians were then Baptists, what kind of churches did they form? Baptist churches, of course.

Ypeij and Dermount (Dutch Reformed Church): In 1819 the king of the Netherlands appointed these men to write a history of the Dutch Reformed Church, and to investigate the claims of the Dutch Baptists that they could trace their history back to Christ. These men wrote in their report: "We have now seen that the Baptists who were formerly called Anabaptists, and in later times Mennonites, were the original Waldenses, and who have long in history . . . received the honor of that origin. On this account the Baptists may be considered as the only Christian community which has stood since the days of the apostles, and as a Christian society which has preserved pure the doctrines of the Gospel through all the ages" (quoted from Christian, *History,* p. 95).

Mosheim (Lutheran): "The first century was a history of the Baptists."

Cardinal Hosius (Roman Catholic): "If the truth of religion were to be judged by the readiness and cheerfulness which a man of any sect shows in suffering, then the opinions and persuasions of *no sect can be truer or surer* than those of the Anabaptists; since there have been none for *these twelve hundred years past* that have been more grievously punished" (quoted from G. H. Orchard, *A Concise History of Foreign Baptists,* p. 364).

4. Whether the historical relationship can be established or not, we can certainly say that Baptist churches of today are New Testament churches, in their doctrine, organization, and practice. It must be our purpose as Baptists to keep them true to the New Testament in every way—the type of churches Christ wants and needs in the world.

III. *A Brief Summary of Church History*

In apostolic days and for a period thereafter, the churches remained reasonably free from false teaching. Even before the end of the first century, however, Satan began to sow evil seeds. Churches here and there were teaching doctrines not true to "the faith which was once delivered unto the saints." Baptismal regeneration, salvation by works or law, centralized church government, union of church and state, and other heresies appeared.

In the year 312 the Roman emperor Constantine took the first steps toward governmental support for Christianity. Gradually, church and state were united into a great politico-ecclesiastical alliance. This union finally culminated in the full development of Roman Catholicism by about the end of the sixth century. With Catholicism in control the Dark Ages came. The period lasted until the Reformation. The translation of the Scriptures into the language of the people, the invention of printing, and revolt of many religious leaders against the Roman hierarchy then brought a new day in world history.

During all this time of the rise and development of false doctrine and practice in the churches, there were scattered through Europe, Asia, and Africa, groups of dissenting churches which refused to acknowledge the Roman pope and sought to follow the New Testament. Some early groups were the Montanists, Novatians, and Donatists. Later groups included the Petrobrusians, Waldensees, and Anabaptists. Catholic historians call most of these sects "Anabaptists." They were mercilessly persecuted throughout the centuries until after the Reformation, and some persecution against them has continued to modern times.

Though these groups did not carry the name "Baptists," many of them did hold various Baptist tenets, such as separation of church and state, spiritual democracy, salvation by grace apart from sacraments, believers' baptism, and immersion as the mode of baptism. Churches holding these truths cherished New Testament principles. They shared with Baptists the desire to follow Christ's will for his churches.

When the Reformation came, numerous new non-Catholic groups appeared. Some of them became the large Protestant denominations of today. They all rejected many of the heresies of the Roman Catholic Church, but most of them retained some teachings which had no foundation in the New Testament. In the centuries since the Reformation other denominations have been formed until there are now hundreds of separate denominational organizations. Some of them have departed far from using the New Testament as their only rule of faith and practice.

In the Reformation period the people called Baptists also appeared. As we have already stated, many historians believe that they had existed under other names in the preceding centuries. Now they became known as Baptists, and their history may be clearly traced from that period. In England, they began a slow but steady growth. Soon they began to appear in other lands. Here in America the first Baptist church was established in Rhode Island about 1738, and soon there were churches in other colonies. They grew very rapidly during the Revolutionary period and the early years of the new nation. Today, Baptists constitute the largest evangelical group in America, with approximately twenty million members. There are now more than twenty-five million Baptists in the world, with churches in more than one hundred nations.

IV. Baptist Past and Baptist Future

Baptists have contributed many things to the world's progress. Perhaps their greatest contribution is religious freedom. They have fought for it through the centuries, and its establishment in America came largely through their influence and effort. They also inaugurated the modern mission movement. William Carey, an English Baptist, was the first foreign missionary of the English-speaking world. The first Sunday school society for Bible teaching was started by a Baptist layman in London, and the great Bible societies of England and America have had strong Baptist support. Baptists have made many other contributions to the progress of Christianity.

The Baptist past is glorious. As we remain true to Christ, our future is assured. The Lord has promised that his churches will be here until the "end of the world." Inspired by the unfailing devotion of our forebears and assured of victory by the promises of God, let us as Baptists, in this day of religious compromise and retreat, hold fast "the faith which was once delivered unto the saints." Let us, with renewed fervor, lift up the banner of him who said, "And I, if I be lifted up from the earth, will draw all men unto me" (John 12:32).

5. Baptist Doctrine

A church is known not only by its history but also by its doctrine. We believe that Baptist origins can be traced back to Christ. We thus should be able to identify the Lord's churches by their doctrines. The Lord's churches today will be teaching what his churches in the first century taught.

We cannot, in a booklet like this, attempt to discuss fully the doctrines of Baptists. Their positions on such matters as the inspiration of the Scriptures, the Trinity, the ruin wrought by sin, the coming of Jesus Christ the Son of God as Saviour, and the future places of heaven and hell are generally known. Some principles strongly emphasized by Baptists have been summarized by J. E. Dillard as follows: (1) Christ is Lord. (2) The New Testament is our rule of faith and practice. (3) The soul is competent in religion. (4) The church is based on personal experience of grace and a regenerated membership. (5) A church is a spiritual democracy. (6) The ordinances are symbols of great religious facts both historical and experimental (adapted from *We Southern Baptists*). In this booklet we limit ourselves to brief outline studies of some of the doctrines held by Baptists that are not taught by all other denominations. We hope the reader will carefully study these with Bible in hand, since the Scripture references alone are used to set forth each doctrine.

I. The Church

1. Christ established the church during his ministry; he was its head and gave it his promise of perpetuity and blessing (Matt. 16:18; 18:17; 28:20; 1 Cor. 12:28; Eph. 5:23; Col. 1:18).

2. The church was a local body of baptized believers (John 4:1; Matt. 28:19; Acts 2:47; 5:14; 14:23; 15:41; Rom. 16:16; Rev. 1:4).

3. Each church governed its own affairs under the leadership of the Spirit; it received members, withdrew fellowship from the disorderly, and restored to fellowship those who repented (Matt. 18:17; 1 Cor. 5:3-5; Acts 15:22; 2 Cor. 8:19; Rom. 14:1; 2 Thess. 3:6; Gal. 6:1).

4. To the church Christ gave the ordinances and the Great Commission, and through it he is to be glorified (Matt. 28:19-20; 1 Cor. 11:23-26; Eph. 3:21).

II. Salvation

1. Salvation is given by God in grace, apart from human works or merit (Eph. 1:6-7; 2:8-9; 2 Tim. 1:9; Rom. 3:24; 5:20-21; Titus 2:11; 3:5-7).

2. It is received by man through repentance and faith. Repentance is absolutely necessary (Matt. 3:2; 4:17; Mark 6:12; Luke 13:3; 15:7; Acts 2:38; 3:19; 17:30; 20:21; 26:20; Rom. 2:4; 2 Cor. 7:10; 2 Peter 3:9). Faith is absolutely necessary (John 1:11-13; 3:16-18, 36; 6:28-29; Acts 10:43; 16:30; Rom. 5:1; 10:9-15; Eph. 2:8-9). This is not just assent of the mind but must be from the heart. Repentance and faith are used together in several places in the Scriptures. (Acts 20:21; Mark 1:15; Heb. 6:1; Matt. 21:32).

3. What is God's plan of salvation? Many different things are being preached. People often say, "I don't know what to believe. One preacher tells me one thing about how to be saved and another tells me another. How can I know which one is preaching the truth?" To help answer this question for the lost and to help the saved to be able to answer it for others, the following test is given. By it anyone can test the plans of salvation taught by men and see whether they are God's plan.

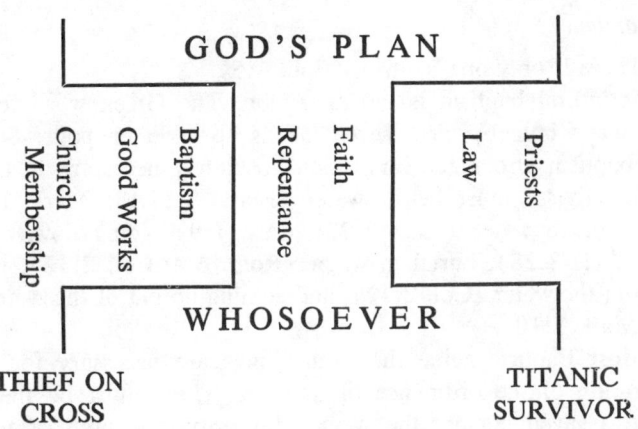

The test is based on the word "whosoever." Revelation 22:17 tells us that "whosoever will" may come to Christ for salvation. Romans 10:13 tells us, "Whosoever shall call upon the name of the Lord shall be saved." John 3:16 says, "Whosoever believeth in him should not perish, but have everlasting life." These passages plainly teach that God's plan of salvation will reach *whosoever*. Since God's plan will reach whosoever, then any plan which will not reach whosoever is not God's plan.

Notice on the chart that the top line says "God's Plan" and the large word below is "Whosoever." Below the "Whosoever" are the words "Thief on Cross," and "*Titanic* Survivor." The *Titanic* survivor is a man who was saved while floating around in the Atlantic after the *Titanic* went down. God's plan of salvation would reach these men, for they are included in the "whosoever."

What plan of salvation preached by men today would reach these men? Could they have joined a church? No! Could they have started doing good works so as to be saved? No! Could they have been baptized? No! Could they have been saved by keeping the law? No!

Could they have been reached by a priest? No! If these things are necessary to salvation, these men had to go to hell. But God says, "Whosoever shall call upon the name of the Lord shall be saved." His plan would reach them. Could they repent? Yes! Could they believe? Yes! They still could meet God's two requirements for salvation.

Use this test. It will show clearly whether the plan of salvation that any man preaches is God's plan. Any plan that will not reach "any man in any condition who calls on the Lord" is not God's plan.

III. Baptism

1. There is only one baptism (Eph. 4:5).

2. Scriptural baptism is by immersion. The Greek word for "baptize" means immerse and never means sprinkle or pour. Scriptures about baptism also make immersion absolutely necessary in the ordinance. Baptism must be in water (Matt. 3:11,13; Mark 1:5). It requires much water (John 3:23; Mark 1:9), going down into the water (Acts 8:38), burial in water (Rom. 6:4; Col. 2:12), resurrection from the water (Col. 2:12), and coming up out of the water (Acts 8:39; Mark 1:10).

3. Most Baptists agree that four things are necessary for the administration of the ordinance of baptism. There must be the proper subject, a saved person; the proper authority, a church of the Lord Jesus Christ; the proper purpose, to show salvation, not procure it; and the proper mode, immersion. Any so-called baptism that does not meet these four conditions is not accepted as scriptural.

4. Baptism sets forth the burial and resurrection of Christ and shows the individual's salvation by death to sin and resurrection to new life in Christ (Rom. 6:4,11). It is an illustration by figure or symbol of salvation (1 Peter 3:21) or putting on a uniform showing that we are saved (Gal. 3:27), done in obedience to Christ's command (Matt. 28:19-20).

5. Baptism is not essential for salvation. There is not one passage in the Bible that teaches that baptism is necessary for salvation. Some passages have been wrongly interpreted to teach it, but there is not one that really teaches it. There is no passage which says "except ye be baptized ye shall be lost." This is said of both repentance and faith (Luke 13:3; Mark 16:16). There are many passages which plainly teach that salvation is without baptism (Matt. 28:19; Acts 10:43; 16:31; Eph. 2:8; Titus 3:5-7; John 1:12; 3:16,18,36; 5:24; 6:35-40).

In the New Testament only believers were baptized, and believers are saved (Acts 2:41; 8:12; 16:31-33; 18:8; Mark 16:16; Matt.

28:19; John 3:16). Paul clearly teaches that baptism is not a part of the gospel message of salvation. In 1 Corinthians 4:15 we are told that Paul had begotten (led to be born again) the Corinthians through the gospel. They had been saved without baptism, for Paul had not baptized them (1 Cor. 1:14-17). Paul also said here that he was sent to preach the gospel, not to baptize. This plainly teaches that baptism is not part of the gospel, but Paul taught in Romans 1:16 that the gospel is "the power of God unto salvation."

6. Every Christian should be baptized, not in order to be saved but because he is saved (Acts 10:48; Matt. 3:15-17; 28:19; Mark 1:9).

7. There is not one passage in the New Testament that in any way teaches infant baptism either by word or example.

IV. The Lord's Supper

1. General references (Matt. 26:26-29; Mark 14:22-25; Luke 22:19-20; 1 Cor. 11:17-29).

2. Consider these questions: Whose is the Supper? It is the Lord's (1 Cor. 11:20). What is its purpose? It is a memorial of Christ's death (1 Cor. 11:24-26). To whom was it given? It was given to the church (Acts 20:7; cf. "general references" above). Who is to partake? Church members are to partake (Acts 2:41-42; 20:7).

Christian denominations generally agree that only the baptized should take the Supper. Baptists do not accept anything as baptism except immersion on profession of faith. Most Southern Baptists also believe that this must be administered by a Baptist church. Churches that do not invite others to partake of the Supper are thus being consistent with their convictions about baptism.

Is open communion possible? No! Paul's statement in 1 Corinthians 11:18-20 shows that open communion is impossible! "For first of all, when ye come together in the church, I hear that there be divisions among you; and I partly believe it. For there must be also heresies among you, that they which are approved may be made manifest among you. When ye come together therefore into one place, this is not to eat the Lord's supper."

Suppose that four denominations are gathered together in "open communion." There are divisions and heresies there, for they certainly do not believe and teach the same doctrines. Paul says that such a group cannot eat the "Lord's supper," for it will not be the "Lord's supper." Open communion is impossible!

How often should the Lord's Supper be observed? There is no command as to this. The Scriptures simply say "as often as ye eat." Some churches observe it yearly, some quarterly, others more often.

V. The Security of the Believer

1. God promises and gives eternal life (John 3:16,18,36; 5:24; 6:47; 1 John 2:25; Titus 1:2).

2. The believer has everlasting life (John 3:18,36; 5:24; 6:47; 10:27-28; 1 John 5:13).

3. Christians do not keep themselves (1 Peter 1:3-6; Jude 24-25; John 10:28).

4. The Christian is hidden with Christ in God (Col. 3:3). If the devil could get us, he would be stronger than God. If he could get one of us, he could get all.

5. We are born the children of God, and we cannot be unborn (John 3:5).

6. Nothing can separate us from the love of God (Rom. 8:35-39).

7. When Christians sin, God chastises them and keeps them (Heb. 5-11; Psalm 89:30-36).

8. Sins of Christians are not charged to them, so they do not have to die for them (Rom. 4:7-8).

VI. Scripture References on Various Subjects

Bible Study: 2 Timothy 2:15; 3:15-17; 2 Peter 1:21; 1 Peter 3:15.

Prayer: 1 Thessalonians 5:17; Luke 11:1-13; 18:1; Matthew 18:19-20; 21:22; James 5:15-16; John 14:13-14; 15:7; Mark 11:22-26; 1 John 3:22; 5:14-15; Philippians 4:6-7; Jeremiah 33:3.

Church Attendance: Hebrews 10:24-25; Psalms 96:8-9; 122:1; Acts 2:44-47.

Soul-Winning: Proverbs 11:30; Ezekiel 3:17-19; Daniel 12:3; Matthew 4:19; John 1:40-45; Psalm 126:6.

Stewardship: 1 Corinthians 4:2,7; Psalm 24:1; Deuteronomy 8:18; Haggai 2:8; James 1:17; Romans 14:12; Matthew 25:14-30.

Giving: Deuteronomy 8:18; 16:16-17; Leviticus 27:30; Proverbs 3:9-10; 11:24-25; Genesis 14:20; 28:22; Malachi 3:8-12; Matthew 23:23; Luke 6:38; Acts 20:35; 1 Corinthians 16:2; 2 Corinthians 8:7-12; 9:6-15.

Missions: Matthew 9:37-38; 28:19-20; Acts 1:8-9; John 20:21; Mark 16:15; Romans 1:14; 10:12-15.

Christian Living: 1 Corinthians 8:9-13; Galatians 2:20; 5:22-26; Ephesians 6:10-18; Colossians 3:17; 1 John 4:7; 2 Corinthians

6:17; 1 Thessalonians 5:12-22; Psalm 1; Romans 12; Matthew 5-7; 10:37-39; Philippians 4:8.

Precious Promises: Isaiah 40:31; 41:10; Psalms 27:14; 34:7-10; 37:1-5; 55:22; 84:11; 91:1; Proverbs 3:5-6; Romans 8:28; John 14:1-3; Philippians 4:19; Matthew 11:28-30.

Death: Psalms 23; 91; 116:15; John 14; 1 Corinthians 15; 2 Corinthians 1:3-7; 5:1-10; Philippians 1:21-23; 1 Thessalonians 4:13-18; Revelation 21-22.

Second Coming: Matthew 24-25; Luke 21; 1 Corinthians 15; 1 Thessalonians 4:13 to 5:11; Revelation; Acts 1:9-11; John 5:28-29; 14:1-3.

Jesus Christ, the living Word, is God's full revelation of himself; the Bible is our only record of his incarnation and atonement. As a summary on Baptist doctrine we thus can say that Baptists accept the Bible as the whole Word of God and the whole Bible as the Word of God. Praying for God's leadership and giving our best effort toward understanding, we seek to teach everything that the Bible teaches. Our doctrines are based on the Scriptures, not on man-made traditions.

6. Baptists and Other Denominations

The world ordinarily thinks of Christendom as being divided into two groups, Catholics and Protestants. This is an incorrect classification, for Baptists are in neither group. Catholicism developed in the early centuries, and Protestantism arose in the Reformation in the protest against Catholicism. Baptists find their origin in the teaching of Christ, given before either of the other groups appeared. Other Christians, however, are here; we work side by side with them in our communities and throughout the world. What is our relationship to them, and what shall be our attitude toward them? In discussing this, two points must be considered.

1. Is One Church as Good as Another?

Some time ago a woman who had been a member of a Baptist church joined a church of another faith. When her former pastor went to talk to her about it, she said, "Oh, well, I don't think it makes any difference, just so you are saved. One church is just as good as another." That statement sounds very nice and seems to be the attitude of a large number of people, but is it true? Let us see.

It is true that salvation is one's primary concern. Every person who has repented of his sins and trusted Christ as Saviour is saved, regardless of his church membership. We believe that there are saved people in all the churches, but all of them have been saved in the same way. If they have not repented and believed, they are lost. When we take the position that one church is not as good as another, we are not talking about salvation.

There are hundreds of denominations in the world today, teaching almost every conceivable kind of doctrine. They cannot all be right, for they do not all teach the same thing. Indeed, many of their teachings are in direct conflict, one church proclaiming a doctrine that another denies. Can both be right? If not, then the one that is right in its teaching must admittedly be better than the one that is wrong.

Five points can be made that will help us to think clearly about this matter.

1. A church established by man is not as good as a church established by the Lord. As we have shown in another section of this book, Christ established his church while he was here on the earth. He promised that it would continue to exist through all the ages until his return. Baptists believe that their churches represent the fulfilment of that promise. Baptist churches, built on the foundation laid by Christ, must be more pleasing to the Lord than churches which must trace their origins back to human founders.

2. Churches that teach error are not as good as churches that teach truth. There are many kinds of doctrines in churches today. Some groups accept as inspired, books that contradict the Bible, the Word of God. Some deny that Jesus was the Son of God. Some deny existence beyond the grave and say that Bible teaching about the resurrection is folly. Can churches that teach such heresies be as good as those that teach truth? Surely not! Other churches do not go so far in their false teaching but do teach doctrines that are not true to the Word. Certainly they cannot be as good as churches that accept and teach the whole Word of God, taking as doctrine only the things taught there. Baptists believe the whole Bible. We seek to teach all that it teaches without one addition or subtraction of truth.

3. Churches that teach only part of the truth are not as good as those that teach all the truth. There are many churches that teach many things that are true teachings of the Word of God. We must contend, however, that churches teaching the whole message are better than those teaching only part of it. Baptists believe and teach the whole Word of God.

4. A church whose doctrines give glory to man is not as good as one whose doctrines give all glory to God. Such doctrines as salvation by works or the believer's need to keep himself give glory to men. Baptist doctrines, such as salvation by grace and the security of the believer, give all glory to God.

5. A church that refuses to obey Christ's commands and takes for doctrines the commandments of man is not as good as one whose sole authority is the Lord. Baptists seek to be obedient to Christ in all things.

We believe that a careful study of these points will convince the reader that one church cannot be as good as another in the sight of the Lord.

II. What Is the Baptist Attitude Toward Other Christians?

The fact that one church is not as good as another does not mean that we cannot have Christian fellowship with all other true Christians. We are united as brethren in Christ with all others who are "children of God by faith in Christ Jesus." There is in our hearts "love toward all the saints," and we sincerely desire that every man shall have the right to worship God as he sees fit, even though we cannot approve the false doctrine he may be teaching.

We believe in Christian unity and long for the day when it may come, but we can never enter into any union that is not based on the acceptance of all the truth of God's Word. Our attitude toward others is not one of arrogance, bitterness, or hostility; it is the attitude of broad, sympathetic love alongside a clear, definite loyalty to Christ and his Word. In that spirit Baptists can mean most to Christ and the world.

7. *God's Plan of Church Finance*

God works by plans. He has a plan for everything. He had a plan when he made the universe. He had a plan when he created man, and he had a plan for the human family on the earth. He had a plan of salvation and a plan for the work of his church. He had a plan also for the financing of the great program that he gave his church to do.

God did not plan for his people to use worldly schemes to raise money for the spread of his message. God nowhere says that his churches are to have sales, raffles, or bazaars to raise money for their work. He did not intend for them to become beggars, going out into the world asking for means to carry on. Such schemes and plans are a shame and disgrace to the church and certainly can never be pleasing to the Lord.

God gives only one plan of church finance in the Bible, and that is tithes and offerings from his people. The tithe is the tenth, meaning that God's people are to bring a tenth of their incomes to the Lord and his work. Offerings are the amounts that are given above the tenth. This is the plan that God teaches all through his Word, and it is the one scriptural plan of church finance.

The key verse of New Testament church finance is found in 1 Corinthians 9:13-14 which reads: "Do ye not know that they which minister about holy things live of the things of the temple? and they which wait at the altar are partakers with the altar? Even so hath the Lord ordained that they which preach the gospel should live of the gospel." Verse 13 refers to Numbers 18:21-28, which tells how the Temple worship and the priests and Levites were supported by the tithes and offerings of the people. All of the people were commanded to bring their tithes and offerings, which were used to support the Lord's work.

Paul's next words are, "Even so." These have the meaning, "In the same way." Paul was saying that church work is to be supported in the way the Temple worship was supported, that is by the tithes and offerings of the people. Even as all the people in that day were to bring their tithes and offerings unto the Lord, so are we to do today.

Other passages which teach that this is God's plan for us are:

I. Tithing Before the Law of Moses

"And he gave him tithes of all" (Gen. 14:20). In this passage we have the record of Abraham's paying a tithe to Melchizedek, the priest of God. Some have said that tithing was merely a part of the Mosaic law. Here we see tithing being practiced four hundred years before the law. Where did Abraham learn to tithe? God taught him! Either the Lord taught him directly or taught some of those who lived before him.

"Of all that thou shalt give me I will surely give the tenth unto thee" (Gen. 28:22). Here we have Jacob's promise to the Lord that he would tithe. This was long before the law of Moses.

II. Tithing Under the Law

1. Tithing was incorporated into the law. "The tithe . . . is the Lord's: it is holy unto the Lord" (Lev. 27:30). If the tithe belonged to God then, it belongs to him now. If it was holy to him then, it is holy to him now. Numbers 18:24,26,28 teaches that the tithe was to be the

means of supporting the priests and the worship. The priests were also required to tithe.

2. Tithing was practiced under the law (2 Chron. 31:5,6,12; Neh. 10:37-38).

3. Those who failed to tithe were condemned by the Lord as being guilty of sin. Nontithers were called God-robbers (Mal. 3:8-9). Malachi challenged the people of Israel to try tithing and see the Lord's blessings for it.

III. Tithing in the New Testament

1. Christ taught tithing. In Malachi 3:1-4 we have a prophecy that the Lord will come and teach people how to live righteously and acceptably. There follows the charge that Israel has robbed God in failing to give the tithe. In Jesus Christ Malachi's prophecy is fulfilled. Jesus taught in Matthew 23:23 that acceptable living includes the tithe and also the weightier matters of the law, judgment, mercy, and faith. In other words, the tithe alone is not enough. We must live right, too. Yet the Lord said that we ought to tithe. Who are we to say we should not?

2. Other New Testament passages teach tithing. The relation of 1 Corinthians 9:13-14 to Numbers 18:24 has already been set out. First Corinthians 16:2 clearly teaches proportionate giving, "as God hath prospered." The only proportion taught in the Bible is the tithe.

Hebrews 7:8 says "And here men that die receive tithes; but there he receiveth them, of whom it is witnessed that he liveth." "Men that die" refers to the Levitical or Mosaic priests. "He" refers to Christ as the fulfilment of the Melchizedek priesthood. As the people paid tithes to the Levitical priests, so now they pay tithes to Christ as the greater Priest. Tithes and offerings are paid to him through his church.

These passages show plainly that God's plan of church finance is for his people to bring his tithes to his house for his work. Everyone who has an income is expected to tithe. "Upon the first day of the week let every one of you lay by him in store, as God hath prospered him" (1 Cor. 16:2). God teaches that everyone is to support his work.

IV. Summary

Here then is God's plan for financing Baptist churches. We are not interested in man-made plans. We believe in God's plans in everything, and we believe that every member of a Baptist church should be a tither, bringing to the Lord a tenth of his income. If we love him, we will keep his commandments.

This plan of finance would meet all of the financial needs of the churches. If every Southern Baptist were to tithe, our income would total billions of dollars a year. That would make possible great advance in church building, in new churches, in missions, in Christian education, and in every area of our work. The personal blessings to the members for their faithfulness as stewards of the Lord would be immeasurable.

8. Baptist Churches at Work

A Baptist church is simple in its organization. It is a self-governing body whose members have equal rights, privileges, and duties. It is probably the purest democracy the world has ever known.

I Officers

1. The pastor is the chief officer. He is a man called by God to preach the gospel, ordained to the work of the ministry, and called by a church to serve as its leader. He must be a man of the highest-type Christian character (1 Tim. 3:1-7; Titus 1:5-9). He is the leader of the church and is to have oversight of the work (1 Peter 5:1-2; 1 Tim. 6: 12,13,17; Heb. 13:7,17). He must study, preach, teach, lead, exhort and reprove (2 Tim. 2:15; 4:1-5) and must one day give answer to God for the way he has done his work (Heb. 13:17; 1 Peter 5:4). He is to lead the church in accordance with the teaching of God's Word. If he is truly a man of God, he will ever be doing his best for the Lord, for the church, and for its every member.

2. The office of deacon is usually traced to the first church at Jerusalem. Seven men were chosen by the church to assist the apostles. The deacons truly were servants of the church, and they are to be that today. They were men of proved character and spiritual interest (Acts 6:3-7; 1 Tim. 3:8-13). The deacons have a major contribution to make in strengthening the spiritual ministry of the church. There were seven deacons in the first church, but this number seems to have no special significance. The number should be according to the needs of the church. In most churches the pastor and deacons meet together regularly to plan and pray concerning the work of the church.

3. Other officers include the church clerk, who keeps the church records; the treasurer, who handles the church funds; the trustees, who hold title to the property in accordance with the requirements of the

law; the choir director; organist; pianist; and church-elected workers in the educational organizations. In some churches there are also paid staff members, such as minister of education, minister of music, or assistant pastor. All are elected by the church and are accountable to the church.

II. Services and Organizations

Baptist churches usually have many activities, including worship services, Sunday school, Training Union, prayer meetings, and missionary meetings. The ministry of the organizations of the church is as follows:

The Sunday school is the Bible-teaching organization. Its textbook is the Bible, and lesson helps are usually provided. It seeks to enlist both the saved and the lost in the study of God's Word. Its teaching sessions usually are held on Sunday morning.

The Training Union is a training organization. The work consists of regular meetings on Sunday evening with programs on doctrine, ethics, Christian history, church polity, and so forth. It also provides a daily Bible reading program, a ministry to social needs, and other activities that help train the member for active service.

The Woman's Missionary Union and the Brotherhood are the missionary organizations. The former is composed of the Woman's Missionary Society, the Young Women's Auxiliary, the Girls' Auxiliary, and the Sunbeam Bands. The Brotherhood is for men and sponsors the Ambassador, Pioneer, and Crusader programs for boys. All of these organizations lead in the study and promotion of missions and stewardship.

Almost all churches have a choir program. Many have graded choirs, providing music training for various age groups.

Every member of every Baptist church should be regular in attendance at the worship and prayer services. To the fullest extent possible, he should participate in the work of the organizations designed for him. Such attendance and participation will promote Christian growth, give training in Christian work, and open doors of opportunity for service.

III. Baptist Churches Working Together

Each Baptist church is independent and under no head except Christ. No denominational organization has any control over any church. Southern Baptist churches, however, believe in, and practice, the scriptural doctrine of co-operation. Baptist work is done on this basis. Churches work together in the following manner.

District associations are composed of Baptists representing the co-operating churches in a county or similar area. They hold annual meetings at which reports from the churches are given and plans for the work are made. Many of them also hold other meetings for promotion of the various departments of work in the churches. Many employ superintendents of missions to direct mission work within their bounds.

State conventions are composed of messengers from the co-operating churches within one or more states. They, too, hold annual meetings. They support a program of mission and promotional work and usually maintain colleges, hospitals, and children's homes.

The Southern Baptist Convention is composed of messengers from the co-operating Southern Baptist churches in the United States. It has an annual convention. It has a Foreign Mission Board, a Home Mission Board, a Sunday School Board, an Annuity Board (to provide protection for ministers and their families), and various other agencies and commissions. It also provides seminaries and has a hospital program. The Southern Baptist Convention supports thousands of missionaries both in America and around the world.

The main support for the mission and benevolent work of the Convention is through the Cooperative Program. This is a budget plan for dividing mission funds, received from the churches, among the various agencies and institutions. Support also comes from special offerings.

Other conventions similar to the Southern Baptist Convention are found in the United States and in other countries.

The Baptist World Alliance is the world organization of Baptists. It does not maintain institutions and agencies but leaves that to the various conventions. It seeks to promote the fellowship of Baptist groups around the world. It holds a world congress once every five years.